I0738567
WHITE PEACH
GARCIA y VEGA
NATURAL ROLLED
SURGEON G
Cigar Smok
Cancers Of The Mou
Throat, Even If You Do Not Inhale.
NTEED FR

say less

by
marcus scott williams

featuring Will Meier, William Toney, Gabrielle Octavia Rucker,
Eliot Duncan

Cover art by William Toney
Interior design by Kassandra Piñero
ISBN: 978-0-578-84245-5

Published by living room collection

*'You focus on the past, your ass'll be a has-what?'**

---

bitter for the first time

i see how bitterness evolves in people, the <u>dictionary.com</u> definition of 'bitter': *having a harsh, disagreeably acrid taste, like that of aspirin, quinine, wormwood, or aloes,* <u>urbandictionary.com</u>* definition: *to be perpetually pissed off,* i been making myself breakfast every morning, stir fry a lil veggies, couple eggs, some jollof, & i be doggin some fancy bread, Earl Grey, cafe setup in the apartment was the best move, 'Julio what's up papi?!' i always think i'd be particularly prone to separating myself in my old age, i can't tell if that would be detrimental to depression or not, there's a major section of me that wants to live alone in the woods, off in the cut in my cutoffs, i'm eating this egg sandwich cuz i'm hungry & i'm not really hungry-hungry, i'm not concentrating on being hungry, i want some cocaine & not because of this emotionality, because it's just been a minute, thought a lot last night about how people're always afforded the opportunity to develop some trauma or unhealthy habits, muhfuckas act like kids got it bad, consider how much worse it can feel being self-aware of all your issues, & how to properly decode & respond to them, shout outs to me, life ain't never not hard it's mad fun though, cold breeze crip walking all over my elbow region, always thinking about what if i start a family by accident w some person i'm not fw, lil mo bitterness, i'm not having sex anyway so like, people i'm attracted to are never sexually attracted to me?, i mean, should i feel bad that maybe some that are i'm not?, how am i supposed to feel fam?, i'm watching this palm frond bloom infronta my eyes, you ever been too absent-minded to get money?, nobody's immune to confusion, i been reacting badly to seeing intimacy, developing jealousy somewhere down the road without realizing, it's uncomfortable, i'm feeling some shame too for the first time, shame of being jealous, shame at reacting poorly, talk to Momma on the phone, tells me my lil brother & his girl broke up, & still living together, (what i was telling you earlier?), Momma makes me smile, on the bus to therapy the middle of the bus accordions & squeaks as if niggers was playing full court basketball in the bus, i'm here for it, fuck it, to be sought after . . . fuck i figured it out!, i wanna pull away & if i pull away too much

---

*Top definition. Posted by Adrian. July 02, 2006. Currently 544 thumbs up to 195 thumbs down.

i'll definitely grow bitter, betwixtthe fingers or into the void, iont wanna grow bitter, i'm tryna fight it i really am, i don't want nothing else to fall thoo these cracks, each time i give in my eye sockets get weighty, iont know what to do, i've thought about just accepting bitterness & that seems unhealthy, the only other option i think i have is in the cut, there's washing in my chest that tingles, can't keep my attention on shit, you ever look up a disorder & feel uncomfortable about how accurate the general symptoms are to your current mind state?, fight-or-flight is some real real, can't talk about shit w many people cuz if i talk about wanting to be taken care of or how much i'm not fucking, they'll be like,

this nigger just want attention,
       this nigger not tryna work,

or i'll get a lil pity fuck, block it w a lil comedy hoping somebody notices issa cry for help, there's an overpouring & i'm finally alone in the living room, everything's cyclical, i wanna take care of people & when they don't meet my subconscious standards i'm embarrassed or sad then ashamed then i wanna do the dash, self-preservation, then i'm not taking care of people, that sweetspot that balance, it's not fair to think that my friendships don't really appreciate me, not as much as i want them too, & see that right there is just trauma again, projecting ass nigger, i can't project onto people like that, people gonna give the way they wanna give, i should be thankful, i am vv thankful y'all can read this, sometimes you need to keep people at arm's length, there's a brazy line between between fingertips & total isolation.

PUSH
DOWN
& TURN
OPEN
CLOSE

SAY LESS THEME SONG

There is only one for me
You have made that possibility
We can take that step to see
If this is really gonna be

All you gotta do is say lesssssss
Don't deny what u feel
Let me surpresssss lil baby;
Open up your mind and yuhh
I'm about to let u know, I'm off dat
dro dro, dro, dro, dro, dro, dro, dro
Nicks of dat
dro dro, dro dro dro dro dro, ah

Loving you has taken time, taken time
But I always knew u was so fiiiine
I recognize the butterflies, inside me, yuh
Since it's finna be made tonight, tonight

All you gotta do is say lesssss
Don't deny what you feel
You don't want plex lil baby;
Open up that loud & flex
I'm about to let u roll cuz
You got dat
dro, dro, dro, dro, dro, dro, dro
I luuh yooou
So, so, so, so, so, so, so
We blow dat
dro, dro, dro, dro, dro, dro, dro
Rollllat shit
Slow, slow, slow, slow, slow, slow, slow
Let's snugg up clooose
(dro, dro, dro, dro)

— Floetry

that last one was for my people who had Black mommas in the early 2000's.

looking down at my torn up cuticles rubbing my hands together like Cool James massaging his top lip w that bottom joint, just anxious waiting for tryouts to begin. y'all ever know y'all were good & realize Life don't care frfr? ignoring my anxious dickhead tryna tell me we gotta pee & i'm like cuuh chill, i'm just nervous. nervous bout missing out on a some crucial practical Life skills shit. math tests & timed tests on a whole conjure ancient trauma. acquire an inch-long splinter in my purlicue halfway thoo the Materials Handling portion of tryouts & haveta thug out carrying this surprisingly heavy 4x8 plywood board until i can pull it out. listening as intently as i possibly can to the next instructor's definition of terms *shy, proud,* & *flush* & drill two boards together & break some edges on a different board. think i'm proficient enough in each area or take instruction well enough to make the cut. i hit the power pack & put $6 on my MetroCard & choose some new Chief Keef to reduce my anxiety. Spike texts me asking why i'm doing a partial vow of silence. i tell her it's because i'm not happy w recent behavioral patterns, we'll see how This Shit unfolds. thinking bout the constant evolution of interpersonal relationships. sharp tap from one singular acrylic fingernail against aluminum or steel; idk what the train car doors made of. nigger don't know shit. biting tf outta my own nails. *look at that tall one* as an adlib. she eating. all the puppets from Roosevelt Franklin Elementary School have perfect rap names. dogs can't make me feel special. my niggers rocking w grunty me cuz they trust imma do me regardless. runs in my leggings. i think for awhile i'm not really tryna hear about the details of y'all personal lives. just gimme the plain. the weather. sumn like what's on PBS Newshour & what's hannnin outside.

leading authority on friendship,

thinking about my first trip to ny and meeting you
and the chaos of trying to be a writer: whatever
trying to be a writer even fucking means. if I had
to say it means anything it's looking at things,
really considering them, in slow glance, in ache
and in deep plushy breath. that's no definition at
all and that's the whole point, maybe.

i guess there's more to nod out with my fingers
punching the ash smudged keys. like tulip bulbs
and charcoal sticks in my green backpack: my means
to memorialize theresa hak kyung cha: author of
the experimental masterpiece Dictee, kidnapped and
raped and murdered the same day her book was published, outside the puck building. where is her
memorial if I don't shove a scene on the pavement
in her honor?

after the puck building I got myself some thick
lines of blow and did four in the hostel bathroom.
then I danced alone at a dive feeling totally decadent getting robbed with $8 beers. my heels were all
blistered from walking aimlessly in new clunky docs
looking for eileen myles or traces of her at st.
mark's place. there are no places to sit in ny that
don't require you to spend loads of money. the few
stray benches are always taken. i headed drunkwards
to another bar. to ludow. I sucked up my last bank
of snow and let the cold fortify my open solitude.
the smiths played and people were loud and touching
each other in polite ways on the round swivels of
stools. I danced alone, as in I was the only body
not sitting. my cunt was all thump thump yes yes.
I circled my wrists. cocked my chin. I am totally
alone I laughed: this is all I've ever wanted.

me and the german psychiatrist i see decided to up
my dose of anti-depressants. he's pretty good and
makes me laugh at myself. there's a thick book behind his desk that reads: 'trust no one' by frank
bauer. after skimming the proverbial dissociative

cringe of trauma I asked him why he wrote a book of
that title, since psychiatrists are meant to scrape
together trust in their patients to fuse a healing
relational safety that many people with trauma and
ptsd simply haven't had the luxury. he said it was
a long story. I'm paying for this time, I said. he
laughed and said that in the office they had a clue
night and he was cast the roll of 'asshole writer'
and one of his friends had a fake book cover made
for him to carry around all night. I thought this
was good material for a book and I told him so. he
sort of flipped the subject and poured me more water
from a glass bottle and said, aren't all writer's
depressed? i scoffed and said that it was absurd to
try and claim everyone was any type of anything.
then he gave me my diagnosis: fh.22. no, he didn't
give it to me right then no I found it neatly print-
ed on my bill. I have major depressive disorder. i
told my family and friends my diagnosis but i re-
membered it as massive depressive disorder. i think
i prefer monumental.

it's good to not feel paralyzingly dark in suicidal
ideation but also weird to think that i'm taking
medicine to get out of bed.

miss your ig honestly but i get needing to fuck off
from scrolling. i spend at least 30min on insta a
day and I've started just not picking up my phone
until 3 hours after i wake up and it's helped get
me writing early in the am.

I get wanting to stay in ny over going to brown. but
you got in? ya know i did the math vaguely: there's
a .0025 percent chance of getting into iowa and
since brown takes only 7 writers compared to iowa's
25 it's .0007 percent change of getting in. fucking
impossible if you ask me. but some writers do, I
guess you did. I guess the only thing more bad ass
than getting into the writing program is to decline
their offer: to choose the shapes of your creative
life as you see fit, to be sensitive to not institutional allotment of value, but to the unwieldy,
punk scope of your very own voice and community.

do you ever also get annoyed with people netting you
as 'experimental'? it's like actually there is no
variable here I'm just typing my crux of feeling.
I'm not experimenting at all. what can I feature but
traces of tugging images I'm lost in gut.

I'm falling in love with a poet I'll call N. my
pillow smolders in lust even in her briefest of ab-
sences. I just wrote this thing about her:

everything is lie till you make it true with touch
i'm sliding with train track now
later i'll tear words I write into fractals and
leaf blow em on my bare walls
damp bed damp skin my cum smeared and rolling in my
words I point at ::
one new word I found for you will
lodge, crinkled in my waves my hair
i side eye the shapes of it ::
it's enormous it's ancient it's the cold pavement
shaded with late rain it's a shaky pendulum thrash
it's every line I read new it's
you

here's to living in found poetics of joy,

featuring Eliot Duncan

make it past tryouts so now i'm re-adjusting my existing structures. text to Laura: *so you see the need for silence. don't know why none of my friends are making me feel special. i know y'all love me but there's been a disconnect that always leaves me feeling extremely lonely especially w you & it's annoying & i don't like pulling away & confusing friends i just don't know if i have the capacity to empathize or anything rn w anyone but myself. idk really. I figure it out eventually. my intention isn't too hurt your feelings. but until I'm not a placeholder I'm gonna say less.* think i want to get taken care of, whats wrong w wanting to take care of specific people? love the textures in decadent ice creams.

shit three times this morning, each feeling better than the last. baby's first art fairs, i think my first. Stunna surprises me & there's a whole lotta gang shit happening at NADA & independent. back at Troop's spot me her & Stunna fw a lil coffee w some orange & hibiscus notes w some lemon coconut cake & a dark chocolate pairing. i wanna spend all night there then again i wanna have the brib to myself, damn i forgoooot Jeron leaving NYC for a couple months tomorrow so i needta see my lil one off. he has a Metro-Card for me. love that nigger. if you not surrounding yourself w people who challenge you i'm not sure what you doing. stomach in anxious knots from starting this program. maybe i'm just excited, maybe it's the excitement of starting new things & not necessarily that i'm anxious i'll fail. my schedule will change dramatically starting tomorrow. gone are my perfect mornings, waking up like 0930 to wash dishes & water plants & throw on the PBS Newshour while i write this new book or work on a sculpture & smoke spliffs w nice tobacco w AK or listen to Teej work on tracks or running or staying busy until post-1700 when it's straight chillin time more smoking & bingeing *Survivor* on the projector. i'll really miss the freedom from Time. at least now i'll have structure & the freedom that comes w acquiring skills to get this fucking paper nigger i'm off this broke shit. astonished at the twists & turns & intricacies Big Life presents. respect Big L. a minute ago i heard a sorta shuffling in the ceiling that sorta sounded like a cicada, i'm still thinking about it cuz the ceiling fell in twice so far in 2018. let it once more & swear imma finesse us some free housing.

there's an aspect of me receiving v lil intimate affection that feels like abject societal rejection & it hurts because my output is unmatched & all i dream about is taking care of people. iont do it for the clout, shit maybe some clout will make it seem as though the decisions i make have value. nothing like a philosophy podcast to somehow make you feel understood.

throughout knowing Big L you'll see parallels of your behavioral patterns. it's up to you to decide what's okay. i get frustrated because i wanna take care of people but the frustration stems from a lack of control i think. i gotta take care of people the way they choose. the snow's so excited about springtime it can hardly contain itself. my muscle memory is far more accessible than my memory memory. everyday is looking like i'll get off at 1600, The Bronx by 1700, eat sumn, do some light housekeeping, bed by 2100. weed on weekends.

fat flakes. get discouraged tryna lay out some measurements. i feel like i'm the only one in class who has lil-to-no practical knowledge of any of these tools & i'm embarrassed & discouraged, not enough to give up. i'm just like damn man. my body can't comprehend going to bed at 2100.

think i'm understanding better & tryna decide if that's the Adderall or not; or rather, tryna decide if the Adderall is actually helping me absorb information properly. i ain't got time to dilly yfm. squeezing the anger into my fist cuz we wasted two hours in class on some public assistance shit when i could have been actually learning something i didn't know. wish i could smoke. tossing & turning & having an internal chat w me about how i can feel myself starting to feel lonely soon so i'm tryna prepare so i don't push away or be accidentally trash & terse to people i'm surrounded by. this is one of those times that just feels like complaining so i'm not sure if i should vocalize anything anymore.

fw my nigger jigsaw. killing fractions. maaad irritable sans pack talk. i wanna say i get heartbroken often but because i'm so sensitive i think that's being dramatic i'm mostly tryna claim it so i can have a deeper connection to Mint Condition. w these silicone earplugs in i can hear the strength of my heartbeats & all i keep wondering is what that final one will sound like & whether or not i'll be able to recognize it.

'imagine being as unwanted as waste, or refuse. i don't fw you so much if i call you refuse.' — AK. so lemme tell you what happened last night. but first imma tell you what's happening now: lil roach clips i'm hitting soon as i'm outta class. last night i lay in bed tryna figure out if i actually have PTSD from abandonment bullshit or from perceived abandonment. several texts:

i will probably need to smoke weed a tiny bit during the week eeem though i don't want too

been having flashbacks & shit

you are here for me btw you do a great job

I'm not sure if this next thought has legs but i think i just feel deeply that the people closest to me will abandon me in some way & it's deeper for different people

idk

i punched the bathroom wall that's prolly a sign of sumn

buuuut more than anything it's just everything is compounded but an uncomfortably high level of anxiety that I'm experiencing changing my schedule & doing school shit & feeling pressure & all that. two palpable stress. on top of everyday shit

so there it is the energy i had had to come out & it was sumn else or self harm which i always realize as a distinct possibility but never have but as i say this there's a box holding my tattoo gun set shout outs Rich Homie it's in my backpack

Okay so with the living room tattoos, we've all been giving em to each other for so long — I mean shit I think Marx has like what 5 or 6 plus from me with the gun by now — that I don't even really stop to think about how reckless that shit is anymore, not ever wearing gloves and just doing it like 5 or 6 plus drinks deep sometimes and shit. Got a problem saying no in general and we're all life's-edge livers and the de facto disclaimer is that I'm no professional but we all have enough fuck shit on us in the first place it don't matter. Until like lately all these lil vaguely known cuties want em all of a sudden, and they don't have lil trash stick n pokes already but like of course I'm gonna give em to em anyways, they fuckin looove it. But it's funny cause like, they're always so sensitive and whimper and shit and I wonder if it's like that just like all the homies have a high pain tolerance or just are better at holding it in or what. Like, I had to run over Marx's neck like 5 or 6 plus times cause I only had singles, not a flinch. But then I'll do myself with it after, cause like I can't have already gotten the gun out and prepped and do somebody else and not just give myself some dumb shit real quick, and the funny part is like in these scenarios, with the lil cuties involved cause life is hella generous right now etc, I'm always like damn, I don't actually like the feeling of it. Like I'm fine with it, sometimes get a little involuntarily jumpy like on my *FUCK COPS* pinky toe stars, but like I realize when life is good and I'm not just on my steadily vaguely masochistic self destruct mode dark shit that actually getting the tattoo is just kinda an annoying means to an end. And so it's funny to me that I fuckin looove it so much when I'm all covered in spilt tears kinda bullshit. Picture on instagram of me after filling up my chest after the most recent big ass heartbreak and I got this blurry half smile and looking at the picture from the future I'm like damn like I actually feel bad for myself, kinda wanna gimme a hug. But anyways that's the only time I remember myself smiling for that period of however many months I was just chompin lil nerd speedballs of xans and adderall every day to make it thru work. You make a trade, is how I think about it. All that self-loathing and just like being fucking haunted by The Sad, you can't just ditch shit like that easy, but you can most definitely trade it for a tattoo. It works every time. Inhale exhale, yin yang baby. It's like any kind of traditional classical self harm except later, when you're happy again and some lil baby got you with your shirt off it's the opposite of the scars being fucked up. Like I mean I was a sad kid and whatever so I can see somebody's arm full up with lil razor kisses and not stare but I mean that's me and I got a high shock tolerance and basically it definitely still ain't a good look. Tattoos on the other hand, most definitely are. So that's why I got the homies their own kits, distribute em around the country, so that whenever anybody is trippin too hard and whatever drugs they got won't calm it down they can run some ink in themselves and let that lil bee sting em and carry their shit away. Or else just drunkenly yolo it up on a whim, either way it's all love baby. *Bzz bzz.*

featuring Will Meier

i forget these black pants got the crotch blown out so my scrotum cold af today. 'get yo raggedy ass off the bus w that bullshit. nasty muthafuckas. that's the problem now.' — woman on the bus in response to the old busted dudes smoking cigarettes in the back of the bus. bus driver makes em get off. i sexually identify as a Cocteau Twins song. this whole time i thought Black Kray was from Florida.

listening to the overhead fan oscillating from the ceiling in the psy-
chiatric nurse practitioners office, tappin my foot to the rydm of
it. they giving me Concerta®. listening to the Arabic in the bodega
& hear "Syria" & "Bashar" & some other keywords that pique my
interest. i'm still not saying nothing.

funny that you can't perceive a panic attack while it's hannin. nothing quite like the camaraderie of hella friends having hella hard
times.

been thinking a lot about how i'm not a sexually attractive person, says history. still sensitive. i have lil room for non-smoothness. it's funny how the days after panic attacks are the clearest days you'll ever have. woodwhippin. i'm lowkey v happy & feel such joy at identifying the term *cross cancelling*. a math-based boost in confidence is v specific. & i'm high, now what? i keep skipping the sex scenes in movies & TV shows.

LITTLE MY RIFT

this morning despondently staring through the center of everything
set in front of me
                bluelight
an amber glass of silvered darjeeling
the riddled arithmetic of the essay's acknowledgements:

*I hope the length of the transcripts deters anyone wanting to use them as
fodder for a top-down analysis the speakers are narrators and interpreters
of their own experiences; they aren't subjects of any study*
                (Derica Shields, A Heavy Nonpresence, 2021)

I have this superstition that discourages me from daydreaming too
much or rather
interrupts the process and so there are many threads left buffering
in the interest of preservation which is to say, however final a feeling I think, nothing will ever truly end with me

faithfulness will be tested insofar as faithfulness can be tested if
you can make it to the tree and back if you can wake from out
under the absence of clocks walk cloaked in your full hypnosis

                        forward

there will be a reward

                I recognize it to be a uncomfortable shape:
not everyone reacts well
when you stand by the coffee pot complaining or, through your
tone, insinuate a looming instability by claiming (quite confident-
ly),

                No, I simply cannot die!

imagine for a moment someone believed in your experience without you having to transcribe it in a book and then defend its con-
tents on a public forum from stranges cloaked beneath whatever
prescribed unreliability they feel most comfortable in

it goes unquestioned, the order of your life and the details in which
it unfolded even the oddities such as the blackout shared with your
sister, or that mishap with the furby on the couch

                    (everything always happening in that one
apartment complex…)

in lieu of television I've know the mirror to be pleasing enough
entertainment
even when I glimspe I'm rarely taking anything in but am happy to
waste my days this way
forever, if I must, seated before myself spilling secrets

      See

it's busy-work remembering myself
remembering how as a child I liked to read music then one day
something like a voice spoke over me
and rendered that symbolism dormant
remembering the frequency in which I was scolded at while adding
numbers or
the never-hum of non-praise for drawing the most perfect (the
most perfect!) hearts

featuring Gabrielle Octavia Rucker

methylphenidate. thinking about how wetness affects color. imagine Tony Yayo gets a Tony. always got an empty cardigan or t-shirt
or a smaller blanket to snugg w if the bed big enough. if i really
cannot sleep at night it's good practice for me to walk around tryna exert energy or push out anxiety. all i fucking talk about is my
mental health.

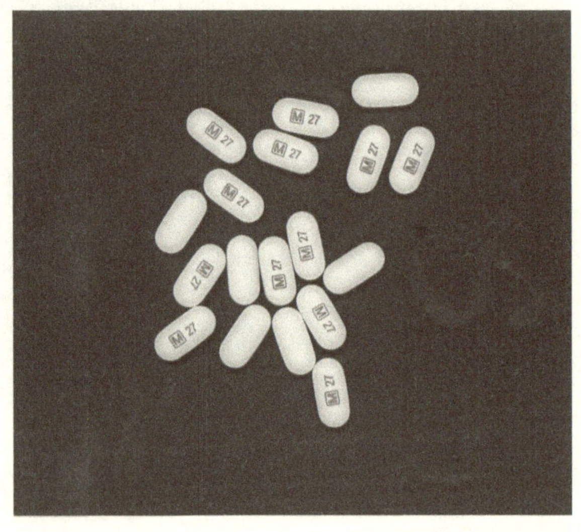

deadassss getting excited about shortcuts to dividing fractions. murder a math test. lowkey the math has been the biggest boost of confidence for me. sumn i thought i couldn't do i do & issa slick lil reminder that when applying myself i can abbomplish these goals yfffm. swear to Gucci i was smiling & having fun taking this math test. i remember as a kid my favorite assignments were worksheets. for me it's like, here's a task, complete the task. shout outs to all the short-term goals i've met & all the worksheets that made me feel like i was indeed adequate as a child. shout outs to that shit stain that ain't tryna go away. i embrace my flaws iont push them away. urbandictionary.com* definition of flaw holding 211 thumbs up: *Something you don't like about yourself and it bugs you. Don't worry everyone has flaws.* my left leg is my strongest leg. i feel the structure in my life settling in in a smooth way sans the fucking getting up at 0530 which regardless of when i went to sleep it's some ol bullshit.

CUT LIST — Small Cabinet Project

Class	Qty	Part Name	Material	T	W	L	Notes
24	2	Sides	Plywood	3/4	9	15 1/8	Edgeband ends & front, rabbet back
12	1	Top/bottom	" "	3/4	9	8 1/2	rabbet back edge 1/2 x 1/2, Edgeband front edge
12	1	Back	" "	1/2	9 1/2	14 5/8	
12	1	Shelf	" "	1/2	8 3/32	8 7/16	Edgeband front edge
		Door	MDF	3/4	9 13/16	14 15/16	Edgeband top/bottom first, sides 2nd, faces last
24	2	Face: In/out	P. Lam	—	10 1/8	15 1/4	
		Face: sides					

*Finished door: 13/16" x 9 1/8 x 10

looking at cool niggers on the train & thinking about how i'm not tryna be a conventionally cool nigger. or a hypebeast is more appropriate term. Steven Tyler is from Yonkers. Yonkers is beautiful. i could retire there. i want it to still be a lil hood a lil round the way spot yfm. 'imagine somebody named Shy-Ann.' — AK.

You know that brick fare is up & down
One minute it's 40 one minute it's 20 one minute it's not around
*You know it's up & down**

* Gucci Mane, 'Up & Down (Free Guwop)', Produced by Metro Boomin,
2013

left my phone at the bribbington all night.

text to Laura: *i was also thinking just now that what i really meant about the done talking, i just wanna concentrate less on talking because i think it could lead to ruminations that could make me super anxious & dissociate but i wanna spend what lil energy i have just living on a day to day basis & keep a monitor on what is happening underneath.* sometimes my texts be beautifully written. this v second it's Sunday March 25 1139 & many seconds & i'm shittin, elbows on knees, chin in hand starin out the closed frosted window thinking, aight i do feel good right this moment.

enthusiastic about catharsis in small moments.

running a lil late today. decide it's worth it to get a lil bagel from Lee's Deli. i wonder about what kind of racism the Chinese woman who's always working the counter in the morning faces while i'm waiting for cream cheese to be slathered on my shit. wonder what the chances are i'll move back to the Midwest. i think the idea of referring to people without money as broke is fucked up because a person's finances aren't the end all be all of living a fulfilling & functional life. i been broke broke since August. i'm still out chere boolin. i feel cute looking down.

been having a solid few days & i'm tryna absorb tryna ppreciate.
the wood-paneled Lee's Deli has a Certificate of Appreciation from
the United States Air Force. is the stock market just a bunch of
suited hypebeasts? i've learned everything that i've always known.

living in NYC reminds me of Big L's temporality. each person i see each & every person i meet there's no guarantee how long the relationship will be or how fruitful. i've lived in opposite places. all the validation i need is a black woman telling me she loves my freeforms. one longboi constantly in my line of vision like windshield wipers on medium leaving lil buffable greasy scratches on my glasses. no school for Good Friday. resumes getting worked on & sent out next week.

staring out of my bay window.

i'm sorry but Dave Chappelle's parody Piss On You may have the hardest hook of all time. Teej's last words as suggested by AK: i can go forever, this shit hard. general Black love out this muuhff man y'all already know what tf time it is! give Ugly God a damn Honorary Doctorate in Music Performance & Composition, a side Master's in English while y'all at it.

i wanna shout out all my organs. iont take advantage of the reliable hair growth. back on my hard boiled eggs & grits diet. shoulders hot in the squad coat. i dig deep for Arthur Jafa's video *Love is the Message, The Message is Death* online, no results. i watch that

conversation w Greg Tate for the whateverth time getting ready.

chewing gum cuz i'm hungry. it's consistently colder in all parts of
Brooklyn.

wake up cranky & cold & looking for tranquility. the greatest April Fool's trick this year was good weather. outside on Park Av i find a brief moment of tranquility that's calming, catching the soft soundless spaces between closely falling snowflakes. snow being compressed underneath these Docs that ain't got virtually any tread left. i think it might be too late to sign up for a lifetime warranty. my go-to fidgeting activity is twisting the dreads & chewing my fingernails round or sometimes chewing the skin around the nails if it's hanging, usually like 1/16th of an inch off that top layer, i gotta watch out or i'll start bleeding & shit or like i'll just be at it for hours & my tips'll be raw. 'two weeks in The Bronx is equivalent to a flu shot.' — a respectable BX native. i'm surprised at the dryness of the sidewalks when i walk out at 1600. hittin roaches at The Set. nighttime & my hood's down & my ears cold & i'm tryna listen. 'it is cuz that's what you did!' week four i'm comfortable enough to sacrifice sleep. it's high fidget hours. real mindrace hours. i've been feeling okay the last few. ppreciate that shit deezamn.

guwoptimism. interesting seeing people bond over which coun-
tries conquered their ancestors. we always find our way back to
ourselves somehow. can't tell if that last sentence was profound or
just some high shit.

is grits a grain? AK whips pancakes w cut up peaches & coconut shavings while i wrist some buttery ass grits w honey & inca sun salt. that stick-to-yo-ribs *liiifestyyyle*'. our new shit at the crib is *House Swap UK*. the shot selection & pacing of the cuts is very 1964 Goddardian. it's perfect. i'm missing the Midwest a bit. i wanna look out over long distances.

still undesirable. my body wakes up shivering because the cold-front in April. can't watch people stories without feeling like i'm not being checked for. these are all neutral statements. watching the fingers turn to hands & arms out my scalp in real time. snack on a slice of wheat bread w some hot sauce. dry af, gotta eat them crustseses eeem though iont want em. see Spitta & smoke against a perfect selfie spot outside the public library across the street from the MoMA. proud of her. Trooop look sleepy but is tryna see the crystals so we all power thoo some hard shit to see the crystals right as the museum's closing. Trooop sings two bars of *Closing Time*. i split at 53rd cuz i'm broke mostly & wanna save the generosity of others for when i really need it. still got grits. brib might be empty. you gotta commit to finishing that yeezy bag for the team. don't travel w that shit leave no child left behind.

it's funny that while chillin w LL earlier i had said that i've never ran into an ex randomly in NYC & then tonight Teezy taps me on the shoulder at Carmelo's. shit is so funny when the universe be listening. i think about her; i think about everybody who's impacted me. we do some light catchup & she tells me she has no plans when she comes back from a wedding back in North Carolina. i wanna be sKCrong & be like naw you slide in my messages if you tryna kick it but like i'm fragile yadidda lonely whatever so given the proper moment i'll reach out. i'm tryna speak at colleges for some gwop tell so y'all professors that *Sparse Black Whimsy: A Memoir* is available on Amazon.

sanding tf out this pine frame i made w 220- then 320 grit paper.
few things are as meditative.

gotta make conscious effort not to use my pinky as a shelf as to protect my ulnar nerve. didn't expect doing any ketamine w Roo the first time we met up & here we are. she's an amazing person & we empath the same way. containing myself until i get that first check yfm. today's the 10 year anniversary of my first instrumental album, *Ahh! Fresh Air.*

staring absently out the hall window at splotches of black base paint covered in silver; the silver shimmers in the overcast, cracking & filling w air bubbles & exposing what's underneath. thinking about inadequacy. routers are my least favorite tool so far. i re-register the CO2 bubbling in the lemon lime Schweppes can. the old re-purposed wood floors crunch underneath each footstep's pressure. lowkey these grits be hitting too y'all sleeping.

tfw you only got $9 in your bank account so you gotta hit the Mc-
Donald's on lunch break cuz they the only place around without a
card limit. i apologize to my organs. i walk around Williamsburg
looking at dormant trees & lil inlets fenced off w barbed wire & i
think of what i could set fire to outta frustration like, who's got the
fucking gall to keep the public away from water. smoke tobacco w
cinnamon tea before during & after Shawnee's set. she kills it after
Zara killt it. talk w Rigo about my friendship documentaries & how
we're collectively responding to the same wavelengths. everything
is vibrations like Roo said. we get to the Maxo Kream show just as
he goes on; my first time at SOBs is cool, the sound is trash cuz issa
rap show & i wonder if rap artists purposely avoid soundchecks.
i feel lonely. there's this realization that i come into people's lives
during transitional periods, hold them up emotionally, become a
pillar; that is until they break out & are ready for the world again,
they back getting they feet wet & i'm marked asexually, like a part of
them. this is such a unique & thoughtful position to find myself in
but i struggle a lot because at the end of the transition period they
see someone new & exciting & approach w that renewed vigor &
i'm in the background beyond happy to have been that comfortable
platform but wondering simultaneously if platforms can ever be a
final nesting place, or is it just a step up the mountain to the next
plateau? my most masculine attribute is that it's hard for me to cry.
it's hard to get excited about meeting new people. Milly been encouraging me to apply to a Master's program at Yale because she as
well as a few random others have said i'd be a great creative writing
teacher & my work has some value & merit & pushes the conversation forward. i hope all y'all are right. i'd definitely use institutional
access to further my goal of starting an artist residency program
for underrepresented artists & to give back always. what's the point
of doing shit otherwise? my hair is soft & the root curls slowly &
loc & hold each other down, fingers become arms. i need to make
time for sleep but this weekend is mad parties & mad people to see
& maybe some lil sumn to creep up on yfm but again i know these
patterns i see behaviors i'm self-aware almost detrimentally so so
how can i get excited? *Heaven or Las Vegas* turned up as much as
it can. i identify heavy w the guitar solo. i pack walnuts & frozen
blueberries in a zip for lunch tomorrow alongside a lemon lime

Schweppes cuz we got it & an orange i opted out of cuz my acid lev-
els are dumb high today. both those snacks remind me ol girl back
in Kansas City summer 2014 whomst is also in Brooklyn currently
w her been-man & hasn't spoken to me since May 8 2015. saw a
picture on Facebook of them kissing & was genuinely happy to see
her face happy. saying 'can't have everything' is corny. feeling thoo
Laura's comforters & sheets in alternating circles w all the lights
shut off & the windows curtained black & the fan on medium dron-
ing heavy on my eardrum to help me sleep. all of this in a panic
frantically tryna find my phone that ended up being safely half-off
the nightstand. i cannot sleep w a shirt on.

unhappiness don't stop me from doing shit. Lil niggers hoopin in
the dark. everybody on the train smiling feet up & shit.

me & Teej plan to set up on each raindrop & punching them niggers back in the sky if they tryna fuck up this smooth lil 80°. new
rap name: Kodak Rxberta.

this the year i'm running back all Max B for the first t. the only way to stop Black people from going to prison is mass diasporic suicide. that's some high shit i just thought. progress isn't automatic w the progression of time. tryna fall asleep w nothing to snugg up to feels like a satellite in space, uncomforted by the Earth not pulling me in; so like i catch it from afar when i can, appreciating it, hoping & fruitlessly waiting for Earth to reach out to me. current long term life goal as laidout in the Bomplicated IG chat: go to Yale eventually receiving a Terminal Master's or PhD in English / film & media studies / sociology / my own madeup shit, teach a class or two in creative writing maybe in skkrealism, use these connections to start a residency program for underprivileged artists who don't have access to materials / facilities / space, most likely in KCMO. who tf knows w that place, then by 60 get a Nobel Prize. 'fuck it i'm just tryna live the most ridiculous life i can" — me to the chat. '*Nobel Prize in rilness*' — Rich Homie to us. fuuuuuuck this Novelist album is so hard.*

* https://open.spotify.com/album/5Ew9BVsDof0qTT6C6tcAV2?si=Dy8XaQgLSWmGz-PivrGU8nA

ACKNOWLEDGEMENTS

yoooooooo i need to shout my peoples real smooth. shout outs the family of course i'm so much like all y'all that i can never stop loving y'all. Myrrh my whole ass heart, William Toney, Rich Homie Will Meier, Joselia Hughes, Stunna, Khari, shout outs Peachcurls we out here breating bontent. my sensei Anastacia-Renee for the encouragement and leaving space in her life for me, Charlie, Charles, Jeron the bag Braxton, Josh Jenkins, Bragg, AK BX all day, the whole Bronx, Shawnee, Chloe, TROOOP YOU'RE OF COURSE MY FAVORITE, Kassssssseeyyy i miss you;(, Milly for the encouragement, catch!, KP, SQ, Sulyiman my G i'm glad we reconnected, Wyatt and Peyton, Greg my mans n nem, Hannah, congratulations by the way, Cris Elie, Shy my fave twin, Nate, Yinka, Simeon, chariot:), everybody whomst follows/'d Run It The Fuck Back or has been to a silent reading of mine, Gabrielle Octavia Rucker, Melissa Spitz, Luke, Jesse, Ashley, Sam, Coleman, Katie, Nikki, Kirby, Lilllllllly, Priscilla, Drew Nutter also conratulations, i would also like to deeply thank to new & budding relationships i've made in the last few years that i'm putting real effort into keeping towards forward my mind: Cheyenne i love you, Elliot, Gina Rodriguez, Hannah Belina, Riley, Lena, Devin, Daniel Owens, Rigo, Zhiwan Chung, noa ryn, & everybody who knows i fw them & whomst's names aren't present, i love y'all, treat niggers w respect, love y'allself, holla at me.

'*Unhappiness will kill yo ass*'
— Sulyiman Stokes

iiight let's get back to it. Chief Keef's *Rounds* & the humidifier poppin. realizing maybe a reason i wanna go to Yale besides the option
that people are encouraging it, is a reason to sequester myself, a
reason to be alone & focus on sumn, that sumn being the intensive
research & writing i'll have to be doing. so at least maybe i won't
feel hopeless & prolly in New Haven i would have a better chance
of living alone. if i'm doomed to feeling perpetually lonely i might
as well be working towards some impossible goal to keep occupied.
i'm looking at this sorta ambivalently. & things always will change
so. i mean i'm writing because it's cathartic yfm? if i get all this out
i can see & perceive the information correctly yfm? how can a person make me simultaneously feel lonely whilst relieving loneliness?
there are subgenres of loneliness. this Life shit. wavy heart gang.

iont know if i should leave or not. i'm glad i am whomst i'm am cuz i'd've cracked if i was another nigger. lowkey all my niggers lonely rn.

think this carrot & guac are old & expired & what else i'm supposed to do? i'm watching myself because i've been thinking about
parallels of me at 19 & i'm really not tryna slip back into flashbacks.
think i'm cool for now. smoke w mans outside Lowe's & after get
dropped off at gas station, dap mans up & walk in grey chilly shit
recording a voice memo about my reactions to the interaction &
about definitions of friendships, my appreciations on niggers concentrating on just chilling, etc. my current outfit — white hoodie
w the hood going up & down, lumberjack flannel w the lil dirty fur
sewn in, dusty ass 511s (shit tbh everything including the dreads
is dusty), matte-rubbed-off Doc Martens, aged white socks, blue
longsleeve crewneck against the body, fingernails red af & chippin
— makes me really crave that face tattoo. keep thinking about a
white ink face tattoo.

today's challenge in mental self-preservation: find a way to stay away from the apartment.

'old people can't lamp, they can only post.' — Flex Trillerson.

always somebody in front of & behind me. i can't see past the future
past this flat robin sky.

still no job offers. processed foods & thermos of acidic ass coffee w whole milk destroying my body. nothingness is an island because nothingness is surrounded by nothingness. love getting crushes often eeem if i might leave pretty crushed. that was wild corny nigger you can do better. no reason for there to be AC on this D.

remember that sometimes you need to be chased rather than doing the chasing. my catch phrase for the last few days has been 'wow what a journey.' just discovered that if i look at myself in the mirror when i'm tripping that i'm such a naturally empathetic person i'll wanna help myself feel better. that last sentence made me smile as much as ctch's smile makes me smile. sitting on Shy's couch i figure sumn out w assistance from a lil DCK: there's nothing that will keep me from being hopeless & feeling lonely or disconnected, so i should just double down on accepting that shit & appreciate the interactions that i get & keep it fucking moving.

'*Fuck trauma lol*'
— text from Flex Trillerson

FULL EMBRACEZ

*the way that i think about love most often
these days is that love is space. it is developing our own capacity for spaciousness within ourselves to allow others to be as they are.*

— rev. *kyodo Williams*, On Being with Kris-
ta Tippet

life here will go on without me. i've become a much stronger chess
player because i've fallen into the habit of voyeuristically viewing
my life like a chess game. i can sense a restructuring in the way i
approach relationships & i'm scared what will happen when i leave
New York & it's not a fear of missing out, it's a fear of waning, some
people falling into obscurity & newer relationships flourishing. no
matter how many times this's happened thooout my shit it's never
easy. tryna react to whomst has me in as a priority in they queue,
eeenat's arbitrary. this has zero to do w friendship status & all to do
w advancing in age & exploring separate paths that may not line
up. if telepathic projection is a thing holla at me so i can rock w my
niggers wherever they at whatever they feeling. Guess FaceTime
could do the trick. there are lil pieces of ya boi left in the dirt like
breadcrumbs. risks become real the closer to action you are. link up
w Shawnee & Anastasia & get some kisses from Owira out in Sunset Park. realize the aforementioned meditations are just reflection
& introspection & are abstract in my present interactions. i'm just
sensitive af fam i need that. Shawnee has designer sunburns. have
to shit in the bathroom right smooth then head to the Chinatown
roof for another final goodbye but i'm shirtless out in my bathroom
cuz it's stupid hot. my GBoard couldn't recognize the word 'button'
what's that mean you think? a few years ago i'd try to pack my day
& fail because i wasn't fully acclimated to NYC rhythms but today
i woke up showered hit the D to Sunset hit Brighton back to the
Bronx stressed cuz i ain't know if seeing Laura would work out but
it clicks boom grab that key & say goodbye on the roof. plus i'm
excited running around after w a Pokemon. get some ice cream.
know i talk mad shit about not believing in time but i've mastered
my own lane & can reliably coordinate plans in several boroughs

within the day. shout outs to me. walking east on Houston St w one hand in my pocket on some quintessential escapist shit. a white woman w a much older man walking a dog, complaining that whenever she coughs she wheezes & i hear the proof. y'all know how i feel about the smoothness of these tires gliding over pavement. sitting across from Katz's, thinking about when i told Pea yesterday that i would never go there mostly because it's expensive but also cuz i'm too good for long lines.

last lil partly cloudy day, the sun is beating on my shoulders thoo my Darkwing Duck shirt headed to the BX to pack. there's a lil bit of me that sees the train ride in few frames. i think about a train explosion while stuck in the tunnels & how fucking funny that would be if i died like that. i got that dissociative stare poppin. call to renew my Medicaid so that's one thing checked off the summer escape list. hot af in the crib gotta shit shirtless yet again. dishes are clean which is nice. email Peter the address to The Set to come thoo tonight. remember when you leave to walk w intent. daydreaming on this 4 train while it's creeping like it's headlights off, daydreaming about creating a writing workshop. feel like my hands are very wise. get off the Bx15 a few stops early & walk the rest of the way to the bribbo. clear royal blue sky. a woman compliments my shirt & i return the favor when i realize i'm jealous of her *Hey Arnold!* shirt. one last dap from the block. find an empty bag of yeezy. it feels almost melodramatic to get mad people together to say goodbye if i'm just leaving for two months. AK talks about it being a very Black thing to tell everybody where you going. 'shit i gotta let y'all niggers know where i'm at cuz i'm not tryna get caught up in no ol bullshit.' on my final dap-hug to Jeron, my youngboy reminds me to remember everything he taught me. 'you taught me how to get the bag.' — me to him.

that's highkey useful.

Eliot Duncan co-created the international queer collective, Slanted House. He's currently writing what the institution calls fiction at the Iowa Writers Workshop.

William Toney is an artist from Kansas City, Missouri.

marcus scott williams is a writer and artist, author of "Sparse Black Whimsy: A Memoir" (2fast2house 2017) and "damn near might still be is what it is" (Noemi 2022). he loves and appreciates you.

Will Meier is an artist and writer turned computer nerd who now makes websites and rave music instead of paintings and essays.

Gabrielle Octavia Rucker is a writer & literary radio experimentalist from the Great Lakes. Her debut poetry collection is forthcoming from The Song Cave in 2022.

photo credit: S*an D. Henry-Smith

Kassandra Piñero is a queer Nuyorican photographer and writer. They are the co-founder of former maga(zine) Sula Collective and the co-founder of B-Roll Press.

Cigar smoking
can cause
cancers of the
mouth and
throat, even if
you do not inhale.
CIGARS FOR
LEAF
VAC
Guaran